You Can't take an Elephant on the Bus

Patricia Cleveland-Peck

Illustrated by David Tazzyman

BLOOMSBURY

LONDON   NEW DELHI   NEW YORK   SYDNEY

You can't take an **elephant** on the **bus** . . .

It would simply cause a terrible fuss!
Elephants' bottoms are heavy and fat,
and would certainly squash the seats quite flat.

And don't sit a **monkey** in a **shopping trolley**...

For monkeys are naughty and find it jolly
to snatch your shopping and chuck it about.
No, leave monkey at home when you go out.

Nor should a **tiger** travel by **train** . . .

Think of the panic. Think of the pain.
Tigers are built to spring and to leap.
Think of the passengers half-asleep.

And don't hail a **taxi** if the driver's a **seal** ...

With such slippery flippers, he can't grasp the wheel.
The taxi will slither and probably swerve,
then throw everyone out at the very next curve.

A **centipede** on **roller skates** is rather bizarre . . .

With one hundred feet, he'd go fast and go far.
But to put on his boots would take him an age –
he'd get in a temper, he'd get in a rage.

And don't put a **camel** in a **sailing boat** ...

It's far too tricky to keep afloat.
His hump and his feet would, I think,
capsize the vessel
and
make it
sink.

A **giraffe** in an **aeroplane** wouldn't be right . . .

The roof of a plane just hasn't the height.
With legs and a neck so bony and long,
a giraffe on a plane would simply be wrong.

And don't ask a **whale** to ride a **bike** . . .

Just imagine what it would be like –
without a bottom to sit on the seat.
And how would he pedal without any feet?

A **pig** on a **skateboard?** Another mistake . . .

He'd be too heavy, it would probably break.
Or his trotters would totter, unable to grip,
and up-and-over the skateboard would flip.

And I wouldn't put a **hippo** in a **hot air balloon** . . .

The basket's too small, there wouldn't be room.
And if it did fly, with hippo's great weight,
it would come crashing down in a terrible state.

And never let a **bear** near an ice cream van . . .

Bears gobble up ice cream as fast as they can.
And if they're stopped they get annoyed,
and an angry bear is one best to avoid.

"Then **how can we travel?**"
the animals shout.
"How can we animals get carried about?"

"What's the best vehicle?
We haven't a clue."

Yes, **animals** on **rollercoasters** are good for a laugh . . .

There's room here for EVERYONE – even giraffe!
So it's goodbye to skateboards, balloons and THAT bus,
for we now have a conveyance that suits ALL OF US!

whee

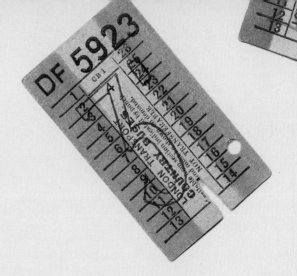

To Isabel, with love ~ PC-P

For Mum and Dad x ~ DT

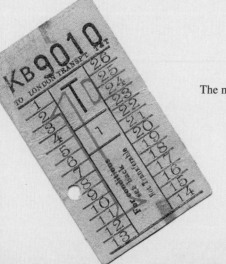
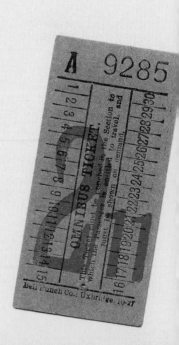

Bloomsbury Publishing, London, New Delhi, New York and Sydney

First published in Great Britain in 2015 by Bloomsbury Publishing Plc
50 Bedford Square, London, WC1B 3DP

Text copyright © Patricia Cleveland-Peck 2015
Illustrations copyright © David Tazzyman 2015

The moral rights of the author and illustrator have been asserted

A CIP catalogue record for this book is available from the British Library

ISBN 978 1 4088 4980 4 (HB)
ISBN 978 1 4088 4982 8 (PB)
ISBN 978 1 4088 4981 1 (eBook)

Printed in China by Leo Paper Products, Heshan, Guangdong

1 3 5 7 9 10 8 6 4 2

www.bloomsbury.com

All papers used by Bloomsbury Publishing are natural, recyclable products
made from wood grown in well-managed forests.
The manufacturing processes conform to the environmental regulations of the country of origin